YOGA ANIMALS
IN THE ARCTIC

CHRISTIANE KERR & LUCY MENZIES

ILLUSTRATED BY JULIA GREEN

Kane Miller
A DIVISION OF EDC PUBLISHING

ABOUT THIS BOOK

In this book, you will read about
Fox's day in the Arctic.

Along the way, Fox will meet friends who will
teach her how to do some simple yoga poses.

First, Fox will learn why each pose is helpful,
and you'll see her try them out.

Then, it's your turn.

Look at the panel at the bottom of each page, like the example below. Don't worry if you don't get it right the first time—keep practicing and have fun!

Read the instructions to follow the pose.

The pictures will show you each step.

CAN YOU DO IT, TOO?

1. Sit with your legs crossed and your hands on your knees. Take three quiet breaths here. Try to notice where your breath starts and where it ends.

2. Breathe in as you bring your hands behind your head, clasping them together, with your elbows out wide.

3. As you breathe out, gently bend forward and bring your elbows to the ground.

4. Repeat three times.

The yoga exercises in this book should be practiced with the help of an adult. It is recommended that children attempt the poses on a yoga mat. For the full benefits of each pose, see pages 30—31.

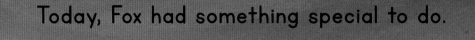

Today, Fox had something special to do.

But she woke up with a funny feeling
in her tummy. What could it be?

"At the start of
every day, I check in
to see how my body
feels, like this,"
said Ermine.

Fox checked in with her body, just like Ermine.

And she realized that the funny feeling was worry.

CAN YOU DO IT, TOO?

 1. Stand up tall with your feet hip-distance apart and your arms by your sides. Breathe in and wiggle your toes. As you breathe out, notice how your feet keep you strong and steady.

 2. Breathe in and raise your hands above your head so that your fingertips touch. Make a balloon shape with your arms.

 3. As you breathe out, gently lower your arms back down to your sides and let the balloon go.

4. Repeat three times.

Because of the worry,
Fox hadn't slept very well.
She'd been tossing and turning all night.

"When I'm
tired, I stretch
up like this,"
said Hare.

6

Fox stretched up,
just like Hare.

And she felt a little
more ready for the day.

CAN YOU DO IT, TOO?

1. Stand with your arms by your sides and your feet wide apart, making sure you feel steady and balanced.

2. Raise your hands above your head. Press your thumbs together, and wiggle your fingertips against each other.

3. Breathe in, and as you breathe out, stretch your arms over to your right side.

4. Breathe in and come back to the center. As you breathe out, stretch over to your left side.

5. Repeat three times.

Fox wasn't quite sure what
her worry was about.

"Moving my body helps
me to think clearly,"
said Ptarmigan.

Fox moved her body, just like Ptarmigan.

And she began to think more clearly about the day ahead.

CAN YOU DO IT, TOO?

1. Stand with your arms by your sides and your feet wide apart, making sure you feel steady and balanced.

2. Breathe in as you stretch your arms out to the side, keeping them level with your shoulders.

3. Breathe out and bend forward. With your left hand, touch your right leg or foot. Let your right arm stretch up behind you.

4. Breathe in and switch sides so that your right hand comes forward to touch your left leg or foot as you raise your left arm behind you.

4. Repeat three times on each side.

Fox's body and mind
still felt a little stiff.

What was different about today?

"I like to loosen
up like this,"
said Walrus.

Fox loosened up, just like Walrus.

And Fox remembered that today was different because she was meeting someone new.

CAN YOU DO IT, TOO?

1. Stand up tall with your feet hip-distance apart and your arms by your sides.

2. Take a big step forward with your left foot. Bring your arms up to shoulder height, with your left arm stretched out in front of you and your right arm behind you.

3. Keeping your arms straight, lower your left arm toward the ground and raise your right arm up behind you. Turn your head toward the center, look forward, and smile.

4. Repeat on the other side. (You can bend your front leg if that feels better for you.)

That's what the worry was!

The thought of meeting a new friend
made Fox feel unsteady.

"When I feel unsteady,
I balance like this,"
said Caribou.

Fox balanced, just like Caribou.

And Fox felt a bit stronger.

CAN YOU DO IT, TOO?

1. Stand up tall with your feet hip-distance apart and your arms by your sides.

2. Breathe in as you press your palms together in front of your chest. Breathe out, shifting your weight to your right foot. Lift your left leg up so that your knee is level with your hips.

3. Breathe in and focus on something ahead of you. Breathe out and slowly lift your arms above your head. Try to balance here for three breaths.

4. Repeat on the other side.

How could Fox feel even less worried?
She didn't know.

"It helps to point
out our worries,"
said Narwhal.

14

Fox pointed out her worry, just like Narwhal.

And as she did, Fox told Narwhal all about how she felt.

CAN YOU DO IT, TOO?

1. Kneel with your bottom resting on your heels and your arms by your sides. Breathe in as you raise your arms and lift your bottom, balancing on your knees and shins. Breathe out and become tall and steady.

2. Bring your arms down, level with your shoulders. Stretch your right leg out to the side, so that your right foot is in line with your left knee.

3. Breathe in as you slide your right hand down your right leg. Breathe out as you stretch your left hand up toward the sky.

4. Notice how you are feeling, then repeat on the other side.

15

Talking about her worry made Fox feel better.
It was good to share her feelings.

What else could she do?

"Breathing in and out helps me
feel relaxed," said Tern.

Fox breathed in and out,
just like Tern.

And her body felt softer.

CAN YOU DO IT, TOO?

1. Kneel down on all
fours. Keep your arms
straight and the palms
of your hands on
the ground.

2. Bring your left foot
between your hands,
planting it firmly to help
steady yourself. Breathe
in as you raise your arms
up. Breathe out.

4. Repeat on the other side.

3. Take a big in breath,
then lean forward as you
breathe out, so your body
and arms point forward.
Imagine you're breathing
out any worries.

Meeting new friends
often made Fox feel shy.

"I do this when I'm
feeling shy," said Whale.

Fox leaned back,
just like Whale.

And she felt
a little braver.

CAN YOU DO IT, TOO?

1. Sit up tall. Bring the soles of your feet together and let your legs drop toward the ground.

2. Lean forward and take hold of your feet or legs.

3. Lean back and try to balance on your bottom as you lift your legs up and slightly apart. See if you can hold this position for a few breaths.

19

It was almost time for Fox
to meet her new friend.

She was still very nervous.

"When I'm feeling
nervous, this is what
I do," said Ox.

Fox focused, just like Ox.

And she knew it
would be OK.

CAN YOU DO IT, TOO?

1. Lie on your back and hug your knees to your tummy.

2. Breathe in. As you breathe out, reach your arms upward and rub the palms of your hands together. Stretch your legs up too, bringing the soles of your feet together.

3. Bring your feet back down to the ground. Rest your palms over your eyes. Stay here for three big breaths.

Fox said
hello to her new
friend, Lynx.

It seemed Lynx felt
a bit nervous, too!

"We could make snow
angels, like this?"
said Lynx.

Fox made a snow angel, just like Lynx.

And it was so much fun!

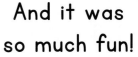

CAN YOU DO IT, TOO?

1. Lie on your back with your arms and legs wide, making a star shape. Breathe in and feel the ground beneath you. Breathe out and notice how your body feels soft.

2. As you breathe in, make your body tight, tensing all the muscles in your legs, arms, and feet. Keep tensing as you count to three.

3. As you breathe out, let everything relax again. Repeat three times.

Fox and Lynx played for hours. They played for so long, that it was almost nighttime.

"I do this after a fun day," said Owl.

24

Fox and Lynx reached for
the moon, just like Owl.

And it was time for the
day to end.

CAN YOU DO IT, TOO?

1. Sit with your legs crossed and your hands on your knees. Take three quiet breaths.

2. Breathe in and raise your arms above your head, bringing your palms together. Breathe out as you settle your bottom into the ground.

3. Breathe in as you stretch your hands up farther. Breathe out as you stretch over to your right side, keeping your bottom on the ground.

4. Breathe in and come back to the center. Breathe out and stretch over to your left side.

5. Repeat three times on each side.

Fox waved goodbye to Lynx.
What had she been so worried about?

"When I'm proud of myself,
I do this," said Polar Bear.

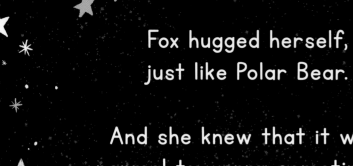

Fox hugged herself,
just like Polar Bear.

And she knew that it was
normal to worry sometimes.

CAN YOU DO IT, TOO?

1. Sit with your legs crossed and your hands on your knees. Take three quiet breaths here. Try to notice where your breath starts and where it ends.

2. Breathe in as you bring your hands behind your head, clasping them together, with your elbows out wide.

3. As you breathe out, gently bend forward and bring your elbows to the ground.

4. Repeat three times.

After her long day,
Fox snuggled down.

She had checked in with
her body like Ermine,
stretched up like Hare,
moved her body like
Ptarmigan, loosened up
like Walrus, balanced
like Caribou, pointed out
her worry like Narwhal,
breathed in and out like
Tern, leaned back like
Whale, focused like Ox,
made a snow angel like
Lynx, reached for the
moon like Owl, and hugged
herself like Polar Bear.

Now all she wanted
to do was ...

... relax like Fox.

CAN YOU DO IT, TOO?

1. Sit up tall, with your legs crossed. Rest the back of your hands on your knees and keep your fingers soft and your palms open.

2. Breathe in as you curl your fingers into your palms. As you do, whisper "breathing in" to yourself.

3. Breathe out as you open your hands up. As you do, whisper "breathing out" to yourself.

POSE BENEFITS

CHECK IN WITH YOUR BODY LIKE ERMINE

- Promotes calm
- Helps with grounding
- Develops breath awareness

STRETCH UP LIKE HARE

- Develops body awareness
- Helps with grounding
- Stretches the spine
- Stretches the sides of the body

MOVE YOUR BODY LIKE PTARMIGAN

- Develops body awareness
- Stretches the legs
- Stretches the spine
- Improves coordination

LOOSEN UP LIKE WALRUS

- Releases tension in back and neck
- Strengthens the legs
- Stretches the spine
- Improves balance

BALANCE LIKE CARIBOU

- Improves balance
- Improves focus
- Develops confidence
- Supports motor development

POINT OUT YOUR WORRIES LIKE NARWHAL

- Improves balance
- Stretches the sides of the body
- Strengthens the shoulders and arms
- Develops confidence

BREATHE IN AND OUT LIKE TERN

- Promotes calm
- Helps with grounding
- Develops breath awareness
- Improves balance

LEAN BACK LIKE WHALE

- Promotes calm
- Relaxes the hips
- Improves balance
- Develops confidence

FOCUS LIKE OX

- Relaxes the hips
- Improves focus
- Strengthens the wrists and ankles

MAKE A SNOW ANGEL LIKE LYNX

- Promotes calm
- Develops body awareness
- Releases physical tension

REACH FOR THE MOON LIKE OWL

- Helps with grounding
- Stretches the sides
- Improves focus
- Improves concentration

HUG YOURSELF LIKE POLAR BEAR

- Promotes calm
- Helps with grounding
- Stretches the spine
- Stretches the shoulders

RELAX LIKE FOX

- Promotes calm
- Supports motor development
- Releases physical tension
- Develops breath awareness

First American Edition 2022
Kane Miller, A Division of EDC Publishing

Copyright © 2022 Quarto Publishing plc

For information contact:
Kane Miller, A Division of EDC Publishing
5402 S 122nd E Ave
Tulsa, OK 74146
www.kanemiller.com
www.myubam.com

Library of Congress Control Number: 2021937014

Manufactured in Guangdong, China TT102021

ISBN: 978-1-68464-241-0

1 2 3 4 5 6 7 8 9 10